Dummy & Me!

Sydell Lowell Voeller

Published by Sydell Voeller, 2024.

While every precaution has been taken in the preparation of this book, the publisher assumes no responsibility for errors or omissions, or for damages resulting from the use of the information contained herein.

DUMMY & ME!

First edition. March 8, 2024.

ISBN: 979-8224456949

Written by Sydell Lowell Voeller.

Chapter One

That stupid old feeling was haunting me again. I knew it was time to strike head-on. Flopping down on my bed, I closed my eyes and for the hundredth time and called forth a picture in my mind. There I was in the school cafeteria with a bunch of kids clustered around me, talking and joking like it was the easiest thing I'd ever done.

My long hair was no longer a dull brown color, but shone with rich auburn highlights. My too-large nose was perfectly formed with just a hint of a ski-jump tip like Sally Murdock's, the most popular girl in the eleventh grade. I wore cool looking clothes with the latest designer labels—not the stuff I'd bought at Goodwill. But the best part of all, I knew exactly what to say at exactly the right times. Even Jason Brennan, the class clown, laughed at my jokes. I had a major crush on him!

The vision suddenly vanished. Negative vibes, the eternal culprit. It happened every time. As soon as I'd managed to concentrate on even a hint of my innermost dreams, there were those vibes, reminding me it was all impossible. My hopes faded as quickly as snowflakes striking a sun-warmed windowpane. During the past week I'd been reading a book about improving one's self-confidence. In it, the author said you had to imagine yourself the way you wanted to be, tell yourself you'd already accomplished your goal, and then live as if you really believed it. Pretty soon you'd discover you were closer to your dream than you ever imagined possible.

I sighed, then shook my head. I'd tried it time and time again. Was it really possible for a sixteen-year-old like me?

Oh, it's not that I lacked friends totally. Tammy Haddon and I'd been best friends ever since second grade. And Delia Zeigler, my locker partner, sometimes joined Tammy and me when we walked to school.

Yet now at Meadow View High School, I wanted to stretch my wings and fibelong to a special crowd.

The sound of my dad's angry voice jerked me from my thoughts. "Dede, how many times have I told you to start dinner before I get home?"

Springing up from the bed, I groaned. "Coming, Dad!"

A couple of years ago, Mom divorced Dad and took off for New York City to become an actress. They had always been so different from each other. My father was contented to keep working at the cannery where he'd landed a job the day he'd graduated from high school. But my mother, who'd majored in drama and graduated from college with honors, was a dreamer.

I know Mom loved my older brother, Bryon, and me. I'll never forget the look on her face that horrible day she told us good-bye, nor my own helpless feelings raging inside. How could she just walk off and desert us?

Still, she was restless, just like her grandfather, a famous ventriloquist in the fifties who traveled with the vaudeville. I could never change her restlessness.

I hurried out to the kitchen, nearly bumping into my father. "Sorry, I guess the time got away from me."

"Deanna, Deanna," he scolded, shaking his bald head. "The time always gets away from you. What were you doing? Lying in that room of yours and day-dreaming again?"

"Sort of." I reached into the lower cupboard and grabbed a handful of potatoes. How could I ever explain to him about my latest attempts at positive action?

"I suppose your brother is working down at the greasy spoon again."

"Dad, it isn't a greasy spoon. It's McDonald's. You know, a cherished American institution like motherhood and apple pie." I'd borrowed those words from a commercial on TV.

He glanced up from the front page of *The Oregon Reporter*. Though his gray eyes looked weary, I could tell my dramatic proclamation had caught him by surprise. Or was it what I said, not how I said it? I wondered a split second later. Why had I mentioned motherhood and cherished institutions? I was only trying to get my point across, not open old wounds.

"Little do you know about motherhood," Dad grumbled. "Certainly nothing your mother ever taught you."

I sighed, saying nothing. It seemed he was always complaining about her.

Before she left, Mom had longed to go to the East Coast. Dad insisted on staying in Oregon. They disagreed about it constantly.

Yet secretly I couldn't blame him for complaining. Why couldn't she have been contented with her teacher's aide job at Blakely Elementary? Wasn't it enough to direct the annual school play and audition for roles at the community theater?

Dad snapped open a can of beer. "Better watch that day-dreaming, Dede. You'll end up just like your mother."

"So? There are worse things than being a dreamer."

I refused to tolerate his criticism any longer and rallied to Mom's defense. Funny how mixed up inside you could feel about someone you love. But Dad would never understand that. He was much too wrapped up in earning a living and hanging out at the Elks Club on weekends to care about me.

Dad clunked his lunch box down on the counter. "Did you get an e-mail from your mother today?" he asked.

I told him I had.

"What's she up to now?"

"She's still stuck in that little rooming house, but she's hoping to find something better soon."

I yearned to be with her, yet I knew it was impossible. She could never afford to keep Bryon and me on her meager income. Dad didn't have extra money to send either.

"You can read the e-mail if you like," I added.

"Later." He dismissed my offer with a shrug.

I glanced up at the clock on the wall. I'd better hurry if I was going to get dinner out on time.

"I hate cooking," I muttered to myself. "Why did Mom leave and dump it all on me?" Now that Bryon had become a senior at the high school and taken a part-time job, it was worse. At least he used to do the laundry in the evenings, but not anymore. That chore had been dumped on me too.

"What did you say, Dede?" Dad's words gave me a start. I hadn't meant for him to hear.

"Nothing," I answered. I shoved the potatoes into the microwave. "No over-time tonight?"

"Nope. The swing shift crew is finally shaping up, so I won't need to fill in for them. Good thing they hired two more men after Jarvis and Kettlemen quit."

The wrinkles in his forehead faded a little, and I saw a hint of a smile on his lips. He rarely smiled anymore after the divorce. I'd watched him grow from a peppy, happy man to a bitter old one. We'd all suffered silently in one way or another, but I couldn't help thinking I'd suffered the most.

"Bryon's getting a raise next week," I said. "They told him that within the next year, he might work his way up to evening manager." I opened a box of Hamburger Helper and dumped it into the skillet of sizzling ground beef. The tangy smells of dehydrated onion rose up about me.

I waited for his reply, but when he didn't answer, I continued, "Bryon's doing a great job there. Don't forget, you were the one who told him it was time he helped with the family finances." I figured that should get a rise out of him.

"Good. That way he can pay for his own car insurance. Next payment's due come April." He gave the paper a quick snap. "The rates are getting just plum out of sight. Why, what with that and the price of gas, pretty soon it won't pay to drive a car, I tell you."

I stirred the hamburger concoction, watching the steam rising from the skillet. "I'll sure be glad when I can get a job. I mean a real one that pays. That way I won't have to bug you for new clothes or money to go to the movies with Tammy."

Every Saturday morning, I took the bus into Portland, Oregon, to the children's hospital. I loved my volunteer job on the orthopedic ward. Lots of the patients stayed there for weeks and weeks, so I'd grown to know them well. It also proved a good escape from my chores at home.

"Tammy still your best friend?" he asked.

"Of course! Tammy and I will be friends forever." Though she'd recently signed up to work on the yearbook and because of that, made lots of new friends, I never doubted her undying loyalty.

"Good." Dad said. "Then maybe Tammy's mother will get you on at the hospital someday." Mrs. Haddon was the activities director there and a lot like a second mom to me.

"She's already talked about that," I answered. "Says I stand an excellent chance of getting hired. Someday soon, matter of fact." I was eager to let him know my efforts could possibly count for something in the future. I'd always wanted to become a nurse for as long as I could remember.

That evening, after dinner dishes and homework were done, a bright new idea popped into my head. I'd try still another plan of attack in solving my self-confidence problems.

I grabbed my diary from the top of my dresser and thumbed through the pages. The blue vinyl-covered book fell open to the last page, exactly where I wanted it to fall open.

Carefully I printed across the top in bold red letters, *My Plan for Positive Action*. In my book, the author had said you also needed to put your goals on paper.

There! It'd be simple. At the beginning of each week, I'd write down a new strategy, sort of adding one on top of the other like building blocks. This first week, I'd concentrate on smiling and saying hi to as many kids as I could, especially kids I didn't know. I wasn't sure exactly what I'd do for weeks number two, three, and so on, but I'd worry about that later.

As I closed my diary, anticipation stirred within me. It was only a matter of time: Great things were just waiting to happen!

Chapter Two

"Deanna, Deanna, don't let the bus leave without me!"

I looked up to see Tammy sprinting towards the bus stop the following Saturday morning. With a long screech the sleek new Tri-Met ground to a halt alongside the curb where I was waiting. The smell of exhaust assaulted my nostrils.

"Hurry!" I yelled as I mounted the steps, but already it appeared the driver had noticed her.

"Kids," he muttered with a grin. "Never on time for anything."

Breathlessly she slid into the seat next to me. Across the aisle sat an oversized lady with a little boy.

"Where're you going today?" I asked. I was pretty sure she wasn't on her way to the hospital too. Despite her mom's persistent urging that Tammy join the small group of high school volunteers, my friend had insisted on doing her own thing.

"Shopping in Portland," she replied with a giggle. "I want to check out that cool resale shop where all the rich people leave their stuff." Her cheeks were rosy from her run in the crisp autumn air and her brown eyes shone with anticipation. "I made a bundle baby-sitting last weekend for the Devlins, and I can hardly wait to spend it."

"That's terrific!"

Tammy gazed at the bouquet of bachelor buttons I was clutching in my hand. "Where'd you get the flowers?"

"From the field behind our house. They're for the nurses."

"Cool! I bet they'll like them." She flashed me an answering grin, but I knew her thoughts were somewhere else.

"By the way," she said, "one of the reasons I wanted to make this bus is because I have to talk to you. And what I need to say is too much to text or e-mail."

"What's up?"

"It's about my mom, actually. She wants you to stop by her office first thing this morning when you get in." The bus again screeched to a stop, and three guys with skateboards climbed on, making their way to the back of the bus.

"Uh—what does she want to talk about?" I asked.

"I'm not sure." She hesitated, biting her lip. "Well, that's not really true. I do know what's on her mind. She wants to talk to you about your ventriloquism."

"My ventriloquism? I haven't done that for ages!"

"She knows that. I think that's what she wants to talk to you about." She darted me a knowing glance. "She wants to convince you to take it up again."

"Be serious!" I exclaimed. A funny sensation fluttered in my stomach. Before Grandpa died when I was around eight, he'd taught me how to do ventriloquism, a talent passed down to him from his father. I'd stuck it out for quite a while, practicing and practicing on a home-made frog dummy I'd fashioned from a big sock.

"I *am* serious," she said emphatically. "That's exactly what Mom has on her mind. She insists the kids on the wards would love it."

I shook my head. "There's no way I could get back into ventriloquism again." I didn't want to tell her how I'd vowed I was done with it forever after Grandpa died and Mother took off.

Somehow, that time hung in my mind like a big empty hole. I realized I couldn't blame Grandpa for leaving, though I felt like it sometimes. But I continued to blame Mom. And odd as it seemed, every time I picked up Ramblin' Rosie—the girl dummy Grandpa had given me one Christmas to replace my frog—it made me think of my mother and Grandpa.

"Remember how you used to get all the kids in the neighborhood together and put on shows?" Tammy asked.

"Sure I remember." The bus driver shifted gears as we turned off the highway onto a busy one-way street.

"You were good, Deanna. Your jokes were funny, and you made that dummy really come to life."

"That was okay then. I mean, we were only in grade school. Of course the kids that age would love it."

"Well, lots of the kids at Children's are grade school age. They'd love it too."

I lowered my voice, glancing over my shoulder at the skateboarders two seats behind us. "You've got to be out of your mind, Tammy. If it got out at Meadow View High School that Deanna Lambert was into ventriloquism, I'd be the laugh of the century. That's kid's stuff. You think I've got problems now."

Thoughts of Mom flashed by me. I remembered the time she'd starred in *Peter Pan* at the theater in the next town. Dressed in her pixie-like green costume, she sang and danced and flew through the air. Everyone raved about her. Yet when she dreamed out loud about being a big star some day, people laughed. Maybe that was another reason why I was afraid of being laughed at too.

"You mean they'd accuse you of playing with dolls or something?" my friend asked.

"Exactly! A dummy, no matter where it came from, is nothing but a big doll."

"Well, er . . . I see what you mean." She looked up, brightening. "But they don't have to know. I'll swear myself to secrecy. I promise."

I stared at her dubiously. "Hmmm, I need some time to think about it." I was certain, despite her promise, the news would still leak out and then wham, everyone would know. Juicy gossip zipped through our school faster than bolts of lightning.

It wasn't long before the bus wheeled into the transfer station.

"See you later," I told my friend as I jumped up from the seat. "Lucky you not having to mess with getting on another bus."

She grinned. "I'll call tonight and let you know if I found any steals."

With a quick wave, I boarded the next bus, then settled back to mull things over. So Mrs. Haddon wanted me to do my ventriloquist bit for the kids at Children's. Was it possible that somehow Tammy was mistaken about that? I doubted it. At any rate, I'd have to decide quickly. In only about twenty minutes, I'd be there.

When I arrived, I headed to the orthopedic ward where I normally worked. Maybe I could stall for time, I decided as I ducked past Mrs. Haddon's office. Turning back, I stole a glance through the big glass windows and noticed with a sigh of relief that she wasn't there.

Good. Maybe I could get through the whole day without having to face her.

"Deanna! Hi!" came a squeaky voice from an opened doorway. "Come here. I've missed you."

Room 302. Six-year-old Misty Ebert. I'd know that voice anywhere. Misty had a hip disease and was one of the kids who'd been in and out of the hospital a lot. With that had come a lot of depression.

I rushed inside. "Misty, how are you?" Reaching down, I hugged her. The sight of her sad blue eyes, bluer than my bouquet, made me glad I was there.

"I'm bored," she answered, dropping her gaze.

I looked down at my flowers, then shoved my hands behind my back. It was time for a last-minute change in plans.

"Which hand?" I asked.

"That one!" She promptly pointed to my right side, and I pulled out the bouquet.

"Oh, for me? All for my very own?"

"Yes, all for you. I'll ask the nurses where I can get a vase. But first, tell me why you're so bored."

"I'm tired of watching TV and working puzzles and coloring and playing video games," she complained. "There's nothing fun to do here anymore."

I pulled up a chair and sat down next to her. "Like me to read you a story?"

"Nah, I'm sick of stories."

Desperate, I scanned the room. An empty brown paper bag, the size I took my lunch to school in, lay on her bedside stand. I flashed it before her eyes.

"Need this for anything?" I asked.

"No, the cleaning lady left it there. She's got lots of them."

As I glanced at her box of broken Crayolas, my thoughts raced. "Here, I'll show you something," I said, reaching for a blue Crayola. "In just a few minutes, abra cadabra, this brown paper bag will become someone special."

Hurriedly I scrawled two oversized blue eyes, then a nose, a silly-looking mouth on the flap, topped with a mop of penciled-in hair.

"Who is it, Deanna? Who is it?"

"A happy clown, named Smiley, who loves to laugh and sing and tell silly stories." Putting my hand inside the bag, I turned and faced my home-made dummy.

"How-do-you-do, ladies and gentleman, I'd like you to meet my friend Smiley the Clown." My dummy dipped into an exaggerated bow. "Good day, Smiley the Clown," I went on. "What's up?"

The dummy stared at the ceiling and answered, "What's up? How should I know! I don't see anything up there!"

The little girl squealed loudly, clapping her chubby hands with delight.

"No, silly! That's just an expression. What I'm asking is—" I heard a stirring from the hallway and looked up.

Mrs. Haddon was standing in the doorway hands crossed over her chest and grinning broadly.

I couldn't help grinning too. I knew then there was no turning back.

Chapter Three

"He-ah-oh, he-ah-oh, he-ah-oh . . ." I was interrupted the following Monday morning by a loud knock on my bedroom door.

"Deanna, what's going on in there?" Bryon asked. His voice sounded mocking.

"None of your business!" I felt my face grow hot with embarrassment. If my brother knew what I was up to, I'd never hear the end of it.

"Oh, come on, kid. Let me in."

I flung open my bedroom door, clasping my hands on my hips. "What do you want?"

He chuckled, his hazel eyes crinkling at the corners. "Just couldn't resist giving you a bad time. Have you found a new way to gargle or something?"

"Of course not!"

"Then what's going on?" he asked again.

I held my breath. "Okay, okay. I'm . . . I'm taking up ventriloquism again." I avoided his gaze as I added, "Tammy's mom wants me to entertain the patients at Children's."

"You're kidding."

"No, I'm not."

"So what's with the strange noises?"

"I'm brushing up on some lip and tongue exercises."

He nodded. "Oh yeah, now it's starting to all come back." He looked a little skeptical, but at least it didn't appear as if he was going to give me a bad time. "You still remember the stuff Grandpa taught you?"

"Well, most of it. But it's going to take practice. Mrs. Haddon already told some of the kids I'll bring Ramblin' Rosie in next Saturday." Just that morning, I'd unearthed the dummy from Mom's old cedar chest where I buried it years ago under a pile of our baby clothes.

"Think you'll be ready?"

"I don't know. I'm going to have to do some hustling." Hesitating, I asked, "Bryon?"

"Hmm?"

I picked at a fuzz ball on my bedspread. "Promise you won't tell anybody about this, okay?"

"Sure, but why not?"

"I don't want them to get the wrong idea about me. I mean, it's just not cool to play with dolls anymore. I'm way too old for that."

He twisted his face in amusement. "Whatever you say, Deanna, whatever you say. By the way . . ."

I lifted Ramblin' Rosie off my dresser as Bryon's words faded into my thoughts. Running my hand over the dummy's face, I felt the smooth plastic contours and saw the blue glass eyes sparkle. A new ache seeped through me. For an instant, I could almost hear Grandpa's merry voice coaching me and my mother's gentle words of encouragement.

My sadness flared into indignation. *Mom, why aren't you here to help me now?* I felt like crying out.

A thud jarred me out of my thoughts, and I realized I'd accidently kicked my positive action book off my bed onto the floor.

"*A Kid's Guide to Positive Action*, huh?" To my horror, Bryon had already picked it up. "Where'd you find that?"

"School library." I'd intended to slip it into my book bag last Friday and return it before anyone saw it.

His grin widened. "So tell me about it."

"There's nothing to tell." Little would he understand. If anything, Bryon's self-confidence was a little too positive. In fact, I'd often thought *Conceit* was his middle name.

"Oh, sure," I grumbled. "As if you really want to know. With all those cute girls hanging on you, I'm sure self-confidence is the last thing from your mind."

"Want a ride to school?" he asked, apparently ignoring my come-back.

"No thanks. I don't have to leave for a half an hour yet, and I need the time to practice. Besides, I promised Tammy I'd walk with her."

With a shrug, he turned and slammed the door behind him.

When I was sure he was well out of ear-shot, I repositioned myself in front of my mirror and carried on. "Who-he, who-he, who-he . . ." I stared at my pouched-out lips, immediately thought of my gold fish, Domino, and I burst into giggles.

"Ramblin' Rosie," I said to the dummy. "Maybe there's hope yet. For the first time in ages, I've pulled you out of the cedar chest. And now I'm even laughing."

* * *

"Look at it this way," Tammy said as we walked to school, avoiding the raised cracks in the sidewalk. I'd been telling her about *A Kid's Guide for Positive Action*. "There's bound to be a pay-off. Since you're feeling nervous about meeting some of the kids at school, you could always practice on your dummy."

I darted her a look. "Hey, that's great! I never thought of it that way."

"Sure. While you practice wise-cracking with your dummy for the patients at the hospital, all you have to do is imagine it's Sally or Kristy or even Jason."

"You really think it will work?" I asked.

"I know it will work!" Her eyes widened with enthusiasm.

I chewed on my lower lip. My friend had a way of making everything sound so easy. Yet secretly I had to admit, it did make sense.

"Sounds like it's worth a try," I agreed at last.

"Good. And while we're discussing great ideas, I have another one."

"Like what?"

"Have you ever thought about signing up for the drama club?"

I hesitated. "Uh . . . no."

"Why not?" We paused at a crosswalk. "It'd be a perfect way to get back into your ventriloquism. Besides, all the kids you've been talking about are members." She ticked off their names on her fingers and added, "Mrs. Nicholson, our principal, always says the best way to make new friends is to join lots of activities. That happened to me when I joined the yearbook staff."

"Don't hassle me," I replied, trying to hide my irritation. "I've got too much to do already. You know how many chores I have at home and what Dad expects of me." Finding extra time to practice with my dummy was bad enough without worrying about joining clubs too.

"Okay, okay!" Tammy said evenly. "Forget I mentioned it."

Inside the school, we parted and hurried to our lockers. I forced a smile, scanning the crowded hallways. Tammy's right, I told myself firmly. If I can joke and talk with Ramblin' Rosie, I can face any of the kids at school.

Kristy, the junior class president, breezed past me. I'd heard she was trying out for the lead role in *Androcles and the Lion*.

"Hi, Kristy," I said, hoping she'd look my way.

"Hi, Deanna!" She waved enthusiastically.

For a moment I was stunned. She'd really answered me.

"Uh . . . good luck with your play auditions. I'll be pulling for you."

Her eyes lit up. "Hey, thanks! You're the first person who's told me that." She smiled as she disappeared around the corner.

I couldn't believe it! It was working. My spirits soared. That afternoon, the very minute I got home from school, I'd write down my progress in my diary. Things were looking up.

At my locker, I twirled the combination, but it kept sticking. Rats! Why did that always happen whenever I was in a hurry? In less than two minutes, the first bell would ring.

I searched desperately for some sign of Delia, but didn't see her. She'd bailed me out of locker troubles at least five times since school had begun, but I could tell today my luck had run out.

From somewhere in the crowd, Jason emerged. Three boys were walking with him. I could hear them guffawing at something he'd said, and he appeared as if he was enjoying all the attention.

A shuffling of feet told me they'd stopped right behind me. Everything went quiet. Suddenly I felt someone—who else but Jason?—press an object against my back. What was going on?

I spun around, my insides trembling, but it was too late. The guys were already at the other end of the hall, tearing past the office like a pack of wild dogs.

I couldn't believe it! Maybe I'd seen a mirage. Maybe as a result of my heavy practice session in front of the mirror, I'd completely flipped out and only imagined what had just happened.

But no, there was this weight still pressing against my back. I reached around and yanked it free. Cardboard!

I blinked. A cardboard sign about the size of a Pee-chee had been plastered to my sweater by three strips of masking tape. On it was printed in bright red letters, *Guess What I'm Doing After School?*

I wanted to die. The news was out. Everyone knew about my ventriloquism.

Hurriedly I slipped the cardboard into my locker and slammed the door shut. My worst nightmare was coming true . . .

Chapter Four

Every afternoon that week after school, I dashed to my room and crammed in some practice time with Ramblin' Rosie. It'd seemed weird working on all those voice box techniques again, kind of like reliving part of my past.

Still, I wasn't convinced ventriloquism was right for me. Performing might have been important to Grandpa and Mom, but being a nurse made more sense, especially if you wanted to be able to pay your bills when you were grown-up.

At least the kids at school weren't teasing me any further about what I was doing. Thank goodness for that! Yet the thought of what they could be saying behind my back nagged at me constantly.

On Thursday, knowing Saturday was quickly approaching, I picked Ramblin' Rosie up from my wicker chair and eyed her critically. Her yellow dress had become a little grimy over the years, but I decided it'd be simple enough to remedy. Maybe tomorrow I'd have time to wash her clothes carefully by hand.

Glancing at my clock on the bureau, I decided there was exactly a half hour of practice time before I needed to start dinner.

I remembered how Grandpa had showed me he could make his voice seem as if it were coming from another place.

His audience, too, had loved the times he'd put his dummy into a big trunk for the closing act, and I was sure the kids at Children's would love it too. Hurriedly I dug through my closet and pulled out my red metal trunk, then stuffed my dummy inside.

Cupping my hand to my ear, I said to my pretend audience, "Listen boys and girls! I hear a voice. What about you?" Next I bent down a little closer to the trunk and said, "What did you say, Ramblin' Rosie? You're asking to come out?"

"Help! Let me out," I made the dummy reply in a muffled voice.

I opened the lid. "Let me out of here!" This time her voice rang out loud and clear.

Over and over I practiced my routines, tossing insults, jokes, and clever remarks to my dummy. Of course, she always tossed them back to me. I was amazed at how easy it was becoming. In fact, I felt so good about my progress, I worked even harder on Tammy's suggestion. If I could pretend Ramblin' Rosie was someone popular like Jason or Sally or maybe Kristy, my problems would soon be over.

I picked up the dummy, positioned her on my knee. "Jason Brennan, why on earth did you make a fool of me the other day at my locker? Just because you're so witty and everyone thinks you're cool, doesn't mean you have a right to pick on kids like me!" I ranted on and on, taking all my frustrations out on my poor dummy.

"Aw, my sweet," my dummy answered. "I fear you misunderstand me. Alas, you're no different than the rest of my friends. You see, I have this one big problem. I'm not the gal you think I am. I'm really an ugly green toad in disguise. And any day now, the wicked witch who cast her spell over me will return and change me back into a toad." My dummy dropped her gaze. "Nothing but a mere toad . . . I have the warts to prove it."

I giggled uncontrollably. This was more fun than I'd expected. Just as I was about to completely crack up, Dad's voice cut through my dialogue. "Deanna? What's going on in there?" He was standing outside my door.

"Just practicing my ventriloquism, Dad."

"Oh, I see. Well, that's good. Tammy's mother is here. She wants to talk to you about next Saturday."

My heart lurched. My room was located not far from the entryway of our house. What if she'd heard all the stupid things I'd said?

A few minutes later, when I was sitting next to her on the living room couch, I lost my uneasiness. Her face beamed, and in her hand she held a bundle of assorted-sized envelopes. "Deanna, I can't begin to tell you how excited the children are about you bringing Ramblin' Rosie to the hospital Saturday. In fact, several of them have written you letters, telling you so." She nudged the letters closer to me. "Here, look at them."

I took the envelopes from her outstretched hand. Immediately I recognized Misty's painstakingly printed name on the outside of the top envelope.

"I thought if I brought these over, it might help you get ready."

I noticed her friendly gaze, her perfectly applied make-up and shining auburn hair. If she'd been about twenty years younger, she'd have looked the way I'd dreamed myself to look during my positive action exercises.

"I guess I can use some help. Thanks for stopping by," I told her. Loneliness for my own mother washed over me. "Mrs. Haddon . . ."

"Yes?"

"I'm really dreading this . . . I mean, it's a lot different now than when I put on shows back in grade school." I shifted my weight. "Besides, I should be helping the nurses with important things, like getting out the meal trays and making beds."

"You *are* helping the nurses, Deanna. Keeping the children happy is perhaps one of the most difficult tasks there is."

"Yes, but performing for them seems so . . . so . . . unimportant." I took a deep breath. "I want to be a nurse someday, Mrs. Haddon. I don't want to be an entertainer like my mom. She never knows where her next paycheck will be coming from!"

She brushed off my argument with a wave of her hand.

"Don't worry. You'll do wonderfully. I have faith in you."

"Thanks," I said, shrugging. I could see I wasn't going to change her mind. "It's just that sometimes I don't have much faith in myself. Oh, it's not that I can't do the ventriloquism, you understand. Actually, it's coming back a lot easier than I expected."

"Good! Then what's the problem, Deanna?"

"It's the way I look, the way I feel about myself, I guess . . ." I hesitated.

"Go on."

"I've been reading this book on positive action," I said. "And the author says you've got to picture yourself the way you want to be someday. You have to do it over and over again till it becomes so much a part of you, you've already believed it's happened."

"That makes good sense to me. Have you tried it?"

"Yes, thousands of times." I gazed again at her well-groomed appearance and lowered my voice. "But let's face it, no matter how hard I try, there's nothing I can do about my big nose and my dull looking hair. I'm sure even the patients at the hospital must think I'm plain." I couldn't bring myself to confess my biggest concern, though, was the kids at school.

"Deanna, that's nonsense. You're very attractive. You might not see yourself that way, but I'm sure others do see it. Then, too, the children adore you. But if the things you mentioned bother you, perhaps you need some motherly advice."

"For instance?"

"For instance, take a look at your posture." With a wave of her hand, she indicated the wall-length mirror on the opposite wall.

I looked and saw my slouched shoulders, my rounded back. "Yeah, I guess I'm not sitting up very straight, am I?"

"No, you're not. Do you realize how much nicer you'll look if you remember to do that? It's so simple!"

I pulled my shoulders back and straightened my rib cage. "Hey, it works, doesn't it?"

"Yes, it does." She paused, studying my face. "You have such pretty blue eyes," she commented. "I'm glad to see you're wearing that lovely blue blouse. It makes your eyes look brighter and bigger."

"Really?" Self-consciously, I ran my hand over the filmy surface of my blouse. Though blue was my favorite color, I'd never realized the color of your clothes could make such a difference.

"Look at it like this," she went on. "If you can make people think your dummy is doing the talking when you're really the one speaking, then by a similar act of illusion, you can detract their attention away from your nose. It's all in how you go about it."

As she talked, I clung to her every word. It was so intriguing!

"Wow, I never thought of it that way before!" I exclaimed. "But what about my hair?"

She tapped her finger thoughtfully against her cheek. "Would you like to go with me to a beauty salon? A professional trim does wonders."

"Oh, Mrs. Haddon, I really couldn't . . ."

"No, no. I'll spring for it."

"Dad would never approve. He wouldn't hear of you paying for it."

"Nonsense! I'll talk to him myself. The hospital gives me a discretionary fund to spend on the volunteers. Let's call it . . ." She eyed me with a smile. "Let's call it a necessity for your debut."

I jumped up and hugged her. "I think you should've been the one who wrote my positive action book!"

She hugged me back. I could smell the faint fragrance of her perfume and feel the warmth in her embrace. Suddenly I was looking forward to Saturday.

Chapter Five

I adored my new hairdo! Under Mrs. Haddon's watchful eye, the beautician had trimmed and styled my hair a special way and recommended using a conditioner. Already I noticed a big difference.

I kept finding it hard to stand up straight though. I had to really think about it all the time. By the end of each day, my shoulders ached from always pulling them back, but I was determined to keep it up. Eventually it would have to change the way I looked . . .

All this to improve my self-confidence! Still, deep down inside, I was excited about what could be in store, so excited I'd almost put Jason's dumb trick out of my mind. Maybe if I at least felt a little better about my appearance, I could handle it at school when the kids teased me about being a ventriloquist.

Saturday morning at the hospital, with Ramblin' Rosie tucked inside her carrying case, I hurried to the nurses' station. The yummy smells of roast turkey wafted from the cart of lunch trays parked against the wall, and someone was paging a doctor on the intercom.

As I entered Misty's private room, I noticed her lying quietly in bed, staring out the window. "I've been waiting forever for you to come back," she whined. "Did you get my picture?"

"Yes, Mrs. Haddon delivered it in person. Thank you, Misty." She'd drawn two stick figures—one large, one small—standing hand-in-hand in front of a spidery-branched tree.

"Who are the two people in your picture?" I asked.

"Me and Auntie Nan."

"Ah, I see."

Scowling, she turned her head away from me and again stared out the window. "Is that your dummy?" she asked when she'd finally again met my gaze.

"Yes. Would you like me to introduce you?"

She sighed. "Oh, I guess so."

I pulled up a chair next to her bed. "What's the matter, Misty? Last week, you loved the clown puppet I made from an old paper bag. Ramblin' Rosie's much fancier. Besides, she's a pro!"

"What's a pro?" Misty smiled faintly.

"A pro is a person, like Ramblin' Rosie, who has practiced something over and over again till she can do it really well. It takes lots of hard work to be a pro." With unexpected pride, I thought about Grandpa, then Mom. For the first time in years, that memory didn't bring tears to my eyes.

"What can Rambo Rosie do?" Misty asked. I smiled, but I didn't correct her.

She tells jokes and stories and makes people laugh. Hold on, let me show you . . ." I snapped opened the carrying case and placed the dummy on my knee. "Good day, Ramblin' Rosie!" I crowed.

"Good day? What's so good about it?"

"Well, that's a fine thing to say. It's good because you and I are here at the hospital visiting some cool kids."

The dummy jerked her head from side to side. "Kids? Kids? I don't see any kids."

"Right in front of you, silly."

Ramblin' Rosie rolled her glass eyes and bowed slightly. "Oh, yes. And who might this pretty little lady be?"

"This is Misty Evans. Misty, meet my friend Ramblin' Rosie."

"Hi," she said shyly. "Are you real?"

This time I hid my smile.

"Why, of course I'm real. And I've got some real jokes to tell too. Are you ready, Misty?"

She burst into giggles, nodding her head.

By the time I'd used up my most recent batch of jokes, Misty appeared much happier. Yet I continued to wonder what had been on her mind that first moment I'd walked in the door.

About half an hour later, her mother came to visit, and I excused myself to continue seeing the other patients. The kids Misty's age gaped with wide-eyed fascination. The older ones wanted to examine all the parts inside an opening in the dummy's back. As I demonstrated the controls that operated her mouth and eyes, then performed short snatches of dialogue, I was surprised to find I was enjoying myself too.

"I'll bring Ramblin' Rosie to the hospital every single Saturday," I promised them. Their beaming faces told me they'd be waiting.

That evening I lay on my bed, exhausted from head to toe. But it was a good kind of exhaustion, the type that comes when you know you've worked hard. I hoped I'd made some of the kids' day at the hospital better, especially Misty's. It must be a real drag being cooped up all the time in a hospital bed.

Stillness hung around me. Bryon was working at McDonald's, and my father had just left to go bowling with some of his friends. Dad had asked me if I wanted to come with them, but I said no. My parents and I used to bowl a lot together in the old days. That was the only thing they ever had in common and only recently, Dad started in again. At least it was a change from the Elks Club.

Grandpa's old clock—the one Mom gave me after he died—ticked from the corner of the room, sounding much louder than usual. Suddenly a blast of music from somewhere outside cut through the quiet.

I ran to the window, yanked back the curtain, and stared at the yard that backed up to ours, Sally's place. In the glow of a full moon I could see a bunch of kids scurrying about on the lawn and several others clustered on the deck. Their screeches and shouts grew louder by the minute.

Muted red and blue lanterns lined the yard, bobbing slightly in the breeze. The beat of the music from inside the house pulsed through the neighborhood. A party. The kind I'd always longed to go to.

Some of the kids were standing around Sally's dad who was busy at the barbecue. I switched off the table lamp on my desk so they couldn't see me standing there.

As I stared into the darkness, that familiar lonely feeling crept in again. I didn't belong. The aching inside me went deeper and deeper. It just wasn't fair.

Unexpectedly I thought about Mom's latest e-mail. She'd written about going to some exciting cast parties. I could just see her, my pretty, maybe even flamboyant mother, laughing and talking to one famous actor after another. What a difference from my humdrum life.

At least Tammy would soon be on her way here to sleep over with me, I thought with a sigh. I wondered if she'd been invited to the party, but turned it down because she'd already promised to be with me. She'd done that once last year and from that day on, I knew she was a real friend.

"Look at it this way," she told me after she'd arrived a few minutes later. This time we both peered through the dark at Sally's backyard.

"If you'd showed up at that party, and someone had asked you what you did all day, you'd probably have been tempted to tell them."

"So?" I failed to see what she was driving at. After all, didn't a lot of them already know about my ventriloquism?

"So you could have blown your secret!" Tammy replied, pulling back the curtain a little farther. "Don't be stupid, Deanna. Everybody talks about what they do on weekends. You could've let it slip without even realizing it."

"Tammy, I think they already know!" I wailed. I told her about the sign Jason had slapped on my back.

"Hmm," she mused. "If that's the case, it's news to me. I haven't heard anyone breathe a word about it."

"Not even Sally or Kristy?" I asked. I wanted to ask about the rest of the drama club kids too, but I didn't know their names.

"No. Not a soul."

"Well, you can't be in every place at once," I said. "Besides, you're my best friend. They wouldn't say anything around you."

Tammy backed away from the window and flicked on my light. "Even if they do know about your ventriloquism, so what?"

"So what?" I echoed. "They'll think I'm a baby—that's what. How am I going to impress any kids if they think I still belong in preschool." I snatched up the bowl of popcorn I'd left on my desk and added, "Tammy, we've been through this before."

"I know, I know. But I still think you're wrong. I bet lots of the kids would agree with me if they knew about it too."

I nearly choked on my popcorn. "I doubt it," I muttered. Just when I was finally beginning to feel good about Ramblin' Rosie again, I'd hit rock bottom.

I wasn't sure what Sally's party had to do with me missing Grandpa and Mom, but somehow it was enough to hurl me back into another dark mood. So much for my positive action.

I stared at the family photograph perched on top of my bureau. Grandpa had taken it with his new camera one Christmas. Mom, looking even younger than I remembered her, smiled radiantly.

"Tammy . . ." I ventured.

"Yes?"

"Do you want to be like your mother? I mean, she's so self-confident and pretty and talented."

My friend hesitated. "Sometimes, I guess. Mom's got her faults though. When I was little, I used to think she was perfect, but now I know better."

I'd idolized my mother too—that is, before she took off.

"Why did you ask me that?" Tammy wanted to know.

"Lately I've been doing a lot of thinking about mothers," I answered. I sat on the bed next to her and drew up my knees. "I can't help wondering if some day I might turn out just like mine."

"What do you mean?"

"Well, already I see myself doing some of the same things my mother's done. When she left us, she left behind the work most moms do.

And every time I take off for Children's to do my own thing, I'm getting out of lots of work too."

Tammy's eyebrows raised. "Are you thinking about running away?"

Giggling, I answered, "No, no. You've got it all wrong. What I'm trying to say is, I'd like to think there could be something special in my life." I shrugged. "My dad says Mom's simply chasing rainbows, but I'm not so sure he's right."

"Maybe not," Tammy replied. "I've never thought much about stuff like that before. Except when she's working, my mother's always around."

I nodded, but said nothing. It felt as if a big black cloud was hanging over me. So far, the only thing Tammy and I'd agreed on about our mothers was that they weren't perfect.

"You going to the Halloween party at school?" Tammy asked.

"Why should I?"

"Come on, Deanna. Don't be a jerk. I've worked my buns off heading up the entertainment committee." She wrapped a strand of hair around her little finger and frowned. "The least you could do is to give me a hand. And just because you didn't get invited to Sally's party doesn't mean you have to be a wallflower all your life."

"Hmm, I don't know." She had a point. Besides, if Mom could have a good time getting out and meeting people, then maybe I could as well. And at least if I was helping, it'd keep me from just standing around looking uncomfortable.

"So what can I do?" I asked my friend after a long pause.

"Lead some of the games. We've got some really cool ones planned."

"It could be fun," I replied, my spirits lifting. I remembered Bryon's old vampire costume I'd stuffed away in the back of my closet and smiled.

What a perfect solution! For a couple of wonderful hours it wouldn't matter even if I were a total social failure. In that disguise, no one would even know it was me!

Chapter Six

"Perfect!" I exclaimed, smudging the last bit of fake blood onto my face. I stared into the mirror, pleased with my Dracula image. My eyes were ringed with black smudges, and white make-up covered my face. I pulled back my hair and tucked it up beneath the hood of the cape. For the finishing touches, I stuck two wicked-looking fangs inside my mouth, but for some reason they kept slipping around.

After readjusting the fangs one more time, I twirled, letting the black cape flow about me. Then I laughed—a deep, throaty vampire laugh. Disguising my voice wouldn't be too difficult, I decided, not after having practiced my ventriloquism so much.

"I see you found my vampire costume," Bryon commented as I made my grand entrance. He gave me a quick once-over and grinned.

"Think anybody will know who I am?"

"I doubt it." He seemed preoccupied. "Hurry, Sis. If you want a ride to the party, we've got to split. Wendy is expecting me to pick her up at eight-thirty."

"Wendy? I thought you were seeing—" The ringing of the phone stopped me.

"Dede, I'm working late again tonight," Dad said after I answered it. "But, don't worry, I'll be out of here in time to pick you up from the party."

"Okay." I paused. "Dad?"

"Yeah?"

"I'm wearing Bryon's old vampire costume. Think anyone will know who I am?" I knew I was repeating myself, but my doubts were getting the best of me.

"Nope. Absolutely not."

"Sure? How can you tell? You can't even see me."

"Look, kiddo, I'll make you a deal." It almost sounded as if he were smiling. "If anyone recognizes you, I'll treat you to two games of bowling.

If no one does, I'll treat you anyway. Now how can you refuse an offer like that?"

"Aw, Dad. I don't know." This was the second time since he'd taken up bowling again that he'd asked me to go.

"Not even if I throw in a banana split at the Dairy Queen afterwards?" he persisted.

I stalled for time, wondering what to say. Why was my father showing so much interest in doing something with me? During the last few years, I couldn't remember a time when Dad and I'd had a real conversation. It'd been easier that way—each of us doing our own thing, staying out of each other's way.

Bryon, who was outside in his car, honked the horn. *Rescued!* I thought.

"I've got to run, Dad. Bryon's getting impatient. Bye!"

Racing outside, I paused to catch my reflection in the hallway mirror. I really looked terrific. But darn those fangs! Why couldn't I keep them in place?

By the time I arrived at school, the party was well underway. In fact, the parents who'd been collecting money and checking student body cards at the front door were already filtering into the gym to join the other chaperones.

I peered inside. Shadowy figures moved around to the beat of the "Monster Mash". The place smelled like a strange mixture of caramel corn and pizza. From the dimly-lit ceiling hung papier-mâché bats. The walls were plastered with everything from jack-o-lanterns, skeletons, and witches to creepy crawly spiders.

Suddenly I froze. I broke into a cold sweat. No one was wearing a costume except me! I scanned the gym one more time to make sure. I had to be seeing wrong—but no, I wasn't. I turned to run. But where would I go? To the john to undress? All I was wearing underneath my costume was underwear.

"Hey, Deanna! What took you so long?" Tammy's voice jerked me from my panicked thoughts.

"Shh! You'll blow my cover!" I shrilled. But it was already too late. At least everyone standing within twenty feet of us had heard her. A couple of girls who were standing close by stared at me and laughed.

"By the way, Tammy." I lowered my voice, turning my back to the girls. "Why didn't you tell me no one was wearing a costume!"

"We voted on it at our last class meeting, remember?"

"No, I don't," I replied haughtily.

She darted me a look. "You were there, Deanna. I know you were."

"Yeah, Deanna." Delia appeared by her side. "You were sitting right next to me."

"Well, I must've been there in body only," I fumed. How could I have missed an important decision such as that? Maybe I hadn't been listening because I wasn't interested in going to the party in the first place. Or maybe I'd been so preoccupied thinking about my ventriloquism and Mom . . .

"Anyway, I think you look cute," Delia said. It was obvious she was trying to be nice to me, but the last thing I felt like being called was cute.

"I'm going home," I told them through clenched teeth. "I feel like a jerk, everyone knows who I am, and I can't put up with two hours of sheer misery." I wasn't sure how I'd get there, but I'd find a way.

"No!" Tammy grabbed my arm. "Stay. I really need your help."

My face flushed beneath my monster's make-up. I felt so dumb, so totally out of it. I was undoubtedly the laughing stock of the entire party. Heaving a sigh, I gave in. "Oh, all right. What do you want me to do?" Out of the corner of my eye, I saw Delia take off.

"Be in charge of the witch's cauldron," Tammy said. "It'll be easy." She handed me a black blindfold. "Besides, maybe the kids will just think you dressed up for the game."

"But I'm a vampire, not a witch!"

"I know, I know. Who cares?" *Nice she could be so nonchalant about this costume bit.* "Okay, what am I supposed to do?"

"The object of the game is to see how many jelly beans you can toss into the cauldron, blind-folded, of course. Each person gets ten tries. Any score over eight wins a bag of bones." She pointed to a big basket filled with assorted bags made of cheesecloth.

I grinned despite myself. "Be serious!"

"I am. It was the parents' idea. They've been saving up old chicken and turkey bones for weeks." She snickered. "If anyone's expecting food for a prize, send them over to the refreshment table."

I twisted the blindfold through my hands. "Got it. Now get lost before my first customer arrives. I want to look like I know what I'm doing."

Expectantly I took my place next to the witch's cauldron, then scanned the gym. Soon three guys I didn't recognize wandered up.

"This is how you play the game," I said, laying on my best vampire voice. By now I was feeling more stupid than ever, but I figured I'd put on a good act. I paused and let out a blood-curdling laugh. Then I projected my voice, making it sound as if it were coming from inside the cauldron. I had to admit, it sounded pretty good.

"Hey, where'd you learn to do that?" the guy in the middle asked.

I shot him an answering grin. "I'll never tell."

He tossed his jellybeans into the cauldron and scored a whopping ten points. Immediately I presented him with his bag of bones.

"Bones!" he hollered. "All this for nothing but bones?" He scrunched up his face.

I was just beginning to feel a little better about this whole thing when some more kids wandered up to the cauldron.

"Look at that dumb costume." One of them laughed, pointing a finger. "Why, it's just like the one my little brother wore to his first-grade party."

I wanted to vanish. I wanted to simply melt into the walls and never come back.

"Who's next for the jellybean toss?" I pretended to ignore their nasty remarks.

"Not us!" They laughed again and walked away.

Glancing across the room, I noticed Sally and Kristy and a bunch of the drama club kids munching on pizza at the refreshment table.

Someone tapped me on the shoulder. "Hey Deanna, how many tries to bring home the lotto?"

"Ten . . . uh . . . ten throws." I turned around and met Jason's gaze. I'd forgotten all about using my vampire's voice, but at least I'd been able to answer him. "That's a cinch!"

I felt like a klutz as I tried to tie the blindfold around his head. My hands were sweaty and the blindfold kept slipping down over his ears. I was sure if I got it too tight, I'd end up pulling his hair or something.

"Ouch! You stepped on my toe!"

I shrank back, mumbling an apology. The evening was becoming a major disaster. Mom's cast parties couldn't be anything like this!

Finally I managed to get it right. Jason began tossing one piece of candy after the other. With little ker-plunk sounds, each one landed directly in the pot.

"No fair!" someone complained. "He's peeking."

"Wanna bet?" Jason pulled off the blindfold in a triumphant gesture.

"So what's the prize?" he asked, turning to me.

Hands shaking, I reached for another bag of bones and gave him one. In seconds he'd disappeared into the crowd.

After a while, the kids stopped coming to play the game. Thankful, I collapsed in the nearest chair.

"Time-out," I said to no one in particular. By now my make-up was beginning to feel like plaster and it cracked whenever I smiled. I glanced down at my watch. Eight o'clock. One more hour to go . . .

"Deanna, you must be starved." Tammy strode up to me with two girls from the cheering squad close on her heels.

"Here, I'll watch the witch's caldron while you go get something to eat. There's plenty of pizza left."

"Great idea." Without a doubt, I'd be just as conspicuous at the refreshment table as anywhere else in the gym, but I was starved.

As I moved across the room, I could feel all eyes staring at me. My stomach growled. I averted my gaze, hoping no one had heard.

"She must've been in detention when we had the class meeting," I heard someone snicker. "She's the only one in this entire place wearing a costume."

"Geez, Thompson, don't be so mean. So Deanna's an individualist." It was Sally answering him. She was sticking up for me. "Here, have something to eat." She handed me a piece of black olive and pepperoni pizza on a white napkin.

"Thanks." My voice cracked. I bit into the spicy wedge. The mozzarella cheese stretched beneath my gaze. I pulled the pizza back a little. The cheese stretched farther and skinnier. I yanked harder, but the elastic strands continued to bridge the pizza slice and my clenched teeth.

A strange hush fell. Then everyone burst into laughter. At first I thought Jason might've had something to do with this, like planting fake cheese in the pizza. But the longer I pulled, the more I realized it wasn't a joke.

At last I reached up and clasped the cheese with my other hand, broke it free and wadded it into my mouth. I was positive, beneath my make-up, my face was glowing in iridescent splendor.

Unexpectedly I felt as if I was going to throw up. I couldn't eat another bite of pizza if you'd paid me a million bucks. As I tossed my remaining slice into a trash can, I looked frantically for the nearest exit. I had to leave. It didn't matter where I went if I didn't stay there.

Turning on my heel, I thought about my English teacher, Mrs. Rosen. She'd promised those of us in her class we'd read Shakespeare's

Comedy of Errors. Well, I had news for her! Everyone here had had a terrific preview from the minute I'd first walked in the door. Everyone but me, of course. I was the only one who wasn't laughing.

Chapter Seven

Every time I thought back to the party, a mixture of feelings swept over me. It was true, as Tammy had pointed out the following day, that Sally had been nice that night. Even Jason hadn't made me the target of another one of his dumb jokes like I'd first suspected.

But still, they had laughed. Everyone had laughed. Maybe they'd thought they were simply laughing *with* me, but I could never live down my embarrassment.

When I sent Mom my next e-mail, I considered telling her about my struggles, but then decided not to. After all, she'd never understand. She was much too busy in her glamorous, exciting new world.

Instead of pouring out my heart to her, I wrote to her about everyday stuff: the weather, my classes, Bryon's new job. It was easier than sharing my real feelings.

As the weeks ticked by, my ventriloquist skills improved. And whenever I spent time at the hospital, I felt confident. At least I didn't have to impress anyone there. I could simply relax and be myself.

I wasn't sure what was making the difference. Maybe Mrs. Haddon's advice about how to improve my appearance had helped more than I realized. Or my continued practice sessions with Ramblin' Rosie really paid off. Anyway, something was working.

On the wards, my Saturdays buzzed with activity.

Besides entertaining the kids with Ramblin' Rosie, I helped the nurses with a million other assignments. Feed the babies, deliver mail, pass out juice and milkshakes at refreshment time—you name it, the list grew by leaps and bounds. But that's what I liked best. Doing practical things.

And above all there was Misty. I'd been so busy, I hadn't been able to spend as much time with her as usual.

Every time I got to grab a few quiet minutes and poke my head into her room, she seemed sad.

One afternoon as I breezed past Mrs. Haddon's office, I heard her call my name.

"Deanna . . ."

I looked up and saw her standing outside the door.

"Deanna, may we talk?"

"Sure. What's going on?" I asked.

"Please come in and sit down."

I eased into the overstuffed chair that faced her desk.

"The hospital staff is planning another big Christmas program for the children," she began. "As activities director, I'm in charge."

"I remember last year's program. It was super."

She peered up over her reading glasses. "Yes, the children always look forward to it. This year, though, we want to try something new. Perhaps put on a variety show for them—like the old-time vaudevilles."

"Oh, sure!" I exclaimed, never suspecting what she'd had in mind. "My great-grandpa used to perform in the real vaudevilles, and my grandfather learned ventriloquism from him." I stopped abruptly, sinking farther into my chair. She already knew that, of course. She'd known it years ago when Mom had first taught me ventriloquism. But somehow, in my excitement, I'd let it all slip out.

Her warm smile soothed my misgivings, and I realized I hadn't needed to be so guarded. "Your grandpa must've been very special, Deanna," she said softly. "Just like you're very special."

"Thanks," I murmured.

"Now, about the Christmas program." She paused to clear her throat. "There'll be a number of people helping out. School groups, community and church organizations. And of course, we want you and your dummy to perform." She leaned closer and rested her chin in her hands. "You will do it, won't you, Deanna?"

I gulped. "Ah . . . er . . . Mrs. Haddon, I just couldn't! I mean, putting on little shows for the kids in their rooms is one thing, but getting up in front of a whole bunch of people is something else." I knew the place would be packed—Moms, Dads, brothers, and sisters plus all the extra performers she'd mentioned.

"Deanna, you sell yourself too short. You've been gifted with much talent, young lady. It's important we take our gifts seriously."

I clenched my hands into tight fists, dropping them at my side. How dare she ask me to do something so scary! Just because I'd agreed to bring Ramblin' Rosie to the hospital one day a week didn't mean I was ready for the big time.

"Promise you'll consider it?" she asked.

"I don't know." My insides were churning like crazy. Maybe my mother felt this way, also, when she had to choose whether to stay or leave. Why couldn't choices be easy?

Though I could see the disappointment in Mrs. Haddon's eyes, she continued to smile. "The date is set for December 10, but I need to know your answer soon—next Saturday at the latest. I'll have to deliver the information to the printers as soon as possible."

All that week, Mrs. Haddon's words kept echoing in my head. Sure, I knew everything she'd said about talent and gifts were true, but the thought of getting up in front of all those people sent me into a cold panic. Talk about pressure! I couldn't possibly go through with it. If only Mom were here to give me advice.

Friday afternoon as I was walking home from school, I gathered my courage and decided to call her. The house was empty, and it'd be a perfect opportunity. She'd certainly be surprised when I told her about my ventriloquism, I thought as I riffled through my pink address book, the one she'd sent me last Christmas. I'd been so careful not to mention my dummy and me in my e-mails. Though I still wasn't convinced she'd understand what I was going through, I was desperate for help.

My heart in my throat, I selected my mother's number on my cell phone. New York City . . . It felt so far away, like the opposite end of the world. Though I'd called my mother about six or seven times since she'd left—mostly on birthdays and holidays—this time New York seemed almost unreal.

The phone rang, but no one answered. I held my breath. What if Mom wasn't there? What if I heard a stranger's voice instead of hers? Without a doubt, she'd made tons of new friends. Maybe there was even a new man in her life . . . "Deanna? Deanna who?" I could almost hear him say. The thought made me ill.

The phone continued to ring. As I waited, my hands grew sweaty. The phone rang again. Silence was my only answer.

Heaving a sigh, I ended the call and sat down to think. What now? I couldn't talk to Mom. I couldn't talk to anyone in my family. I propped my head in my hands and stared down at the tear-drop patterns in the living room carpet. It made me think that crying might help. Yet somehow, the tears wouldn't come. Maybe I was already too cried-out.

At last an idea jolted me into action. All I'd have to do was quit my job at Children's and stay away from Tammy for a while too. Then no one would force me to do something I couldn't handle.

I dashed to my room and began searching for the box of note cards I'd stuck somewhere in my desk. It was a birthday gift from Tammy. After I found it crammed in the back of the bottom drawer, I sat down and began writing a letter to Mrs. Haddon. I couldn't bear to tell her in person.

Pushing back my nagging guilt, I shrugged hurriedly into my denim jacket and prepared to take off for the post office. I simply had to make it in time for the final pick-up. The sooner I got it there, the less chance I'd have to change my mind.

I glanced at my watch. Five-thirty. Dad always expected his dinner to be on the table at six sharp. *Too bad,* I thought. For once, dinner would have to wait.

I slammed the front door behind me and dashed down our street past white clapboard homes. Clutching the letter, I peered down at it. My declaration of independence, I vowed happily. Soon I'd be free. From now on, no one could make me do anything I didn't want to. The nippy autumn air stung my cheeks. Lights inside the houses blinked on, one after another, as the coming dusk settled in. A thick fog crept in, settling over the empty field across the street like a cold damp blanket. I shivered against the chill.

Faster and faster I walked. Two kids on bikes whizzed by, nearly running me down. In minutes, I was sprinting. My breath made wispy puffs of vapor. Leaves crunched beneath my feet. My heart was beating like a crazy drum.

Without warning, I heard the blast of a car horn from behind. I spun around and peered into the gray evening haze. Headlights blinded my eyes.

In a split second, my brother screeched to a halt in the middle of the empty street.

"Deanna!" he shouted. "Where're you going? I've been looking all over for you!"

"To the post office. Don't hassle me, Bryon. It's important I get there. Right away!" I turned again and continued walking.

I could hear him start up the car. Then he was cruising alongside of me. Through the opened car window, he yelled, "Listen up, Sis! I've got something to tell you. Get in the car."

"Forget it! Besides, since when have you become so concerned about me?"

His voice grew stern. "Deanna Lambert, if you don't—"

"Hey," I broke in. "Don't you have better things to do on your night off besides bugging your sister?" I skipped over a fallen branch on the sidewalk, nearly falling flat on my face.

"Look, I don't know what's so darned important. If you get in the car, I can drive you to the post office."

Approaching an intersection, I stopped and looked over at him skeptically. "Fat chance of getting any rides from you. You'll probably just take me straight home to start your precious dinner. I swear, Bryon Lambert, you and Dad are just alike."

"Okay, that does it! You're going to listen to me if it's the last thing you do." He stopped the car by the side of the road, flung open the door and jumped outside.

"Tammy's mom has been trying to get in touch with you. Haven't you checked your phone messages?"

My stomach dropped. Lately Mrs. Haddon always wanted to talk to me. "No, as a matter of fact, I haven't checked my messages," I answered. "I've been much too busy doing other things," I added importantly, tipping my chin.

"Well, as I said, she needs to talk to you. When you didn't get back to her, she called me."

"I know what she wants. She's bugging me for an answer about her stupid old talent show. She's probably working late to get it all planned."

He cocked his head. "Talent show? Heck, no! At least that's not what she said to me."

"Okay, then what did she say?"

"Something weird's going on with one of the patients on the orthopedic ward."

I gasped. "Misty?"

"Yeah, Misty."

Chapter Eight

"Is it something terrible? Won't Misty get well?" I asked Mrs. Haddon from inside Bryon's car. I gripped my phone tightly in anticipation. The lump in my throat was growing larger by the second.

"No, No! I didn't mean to alarm you, Deanna. We've known for a long time that Misty will need another operation. There's no reason why she won't pull through with flying colors."

My shoulders went limp with relief. "Then what's the problem?" I couldn't understand why she was making this sound like such a big deal. I glanced over at Bryon who was sitting still as a statute, apparently in no hurry to leave. The car continued to idle.

"It's her moodiness," Mrs. Haddon replied. "She constantly stares out the window, cries for no apparent reason, refuses to eat, and will hardly talk to anyone." She paused. "This afternoon when her mother came in to visit, Misty was worse than ever. The poor woman's extremely upset."

"Can't any of the nurses get through to Misty?" I asked. A weird feeling crept over me. How could I tell Mrs. Haddon I wasn't coming back anymore? Especially now.

"So far, no one can get Misty to talk. That's why I called. The two of you are so close."

Bryon started up the car again. "Yes, we are," I said, "but . . . but I've just finished writing this—"

"We can't let this go on any longer," she interrupted. "Deanna, can you come in and see Misty? Tonight?"

"Sure." At that point, I had no choice.

"Your dad probably doesn't want you riding the bus so far out of town at night. I'll drive in and get you."

"No, don't bother." I sent Bryon a sidelong glance. "My brother can do it."

After a quick call to Dad to tell him where we were going, we took off.

By then my stomach was growling with hunger, but I didn't care. As we whizzed past the post office, I shoved the letter deep into my jacket pocket. I'd come so close to mailing it. But now I wasn't so sure I still wanted to.

"Hey, wait a minute!" I yelled. Suddenly I remembered Ramblin' Rosie. "Go back home. I've forgotten something!"

Bryon darted me an irritated look. "How about your head, Deanna?" he said.

"Bryon!" I hissed. "This is no time for insults!"

"Okay, okay." He skidded into an empty alley, turned around, and pitched back onto the highway.

At home, I ran straight for the living room where I'd left Ramblin' Rosie on the floor, propped up against the couch. I flicked on the light switch, almost tripping over the vacuum cleaner someone had left alongside the coffee table.

I looked at the couch and blinked. Ramblin' Rosie wasn't there! Had I been mistaken? Was she in my room instead?

Dashing down the hall, I heard Bryon rev the car motor. His earlier patience had flown out the window!

"Hold on!" I shouted, though I knew he couldn't hear me. "I'll be there in a sec."

Inside my room, I scrambled first through my closet, then tossed back the blankets on my unmade bed. I gulped. Ramblin' Rosie was nowhere to be found!

Hurriedly I rummaged through Bryon's room—he'd kill me if he knew that—then searched through the rest of the house. Still no dummy!

My throat tightened as I envisioned Misty, teary-eyed in her hospital bed and Mrs. Haddon waiting anxiously in her office. I could go to them empty-handed, but now I knew how important Ramblin' Rosie was. I was sure I couldn't get through to Misty without her. Unexpectedly I thought again about the vacuum cleaner. Who'd left it there? It certainly wasn't me. I hadn't cleaned the house for almost two weeks!

Then a horrible idea struck me. What if Dad had hired someone to do the cleaning? That was the last thing we could afford.

As I shoved guilt to the back of my mind, I thought about the times I'd vacuumed. Sometimes I moved things around a little so I could do a better job. Like getting into corners and underneath furniture.

I snapped my fingers. That's it! That had to be my answer! Whoever had vacuumed probably moved him just a few feet away.

Outside, I heard Bryon honking, but I tried not to let it get to me. My brother wouldn't have to wait much longer.

I dashed back to the living room and zeroed in on the couch. There alongside it, on top of the magazine rack, was Ramblin' Rosie.

Giving out a small cry of relief, I snatched her up—there wasn't time to bother with the carrying case—and sped back to the car.

"Man alive, what took you so long?" Bryon asked irritably.

"I'll tell you! I'll tell you! Just get going. We've already wasted enough time."

As we tore out the driveway, I explained what had happened.

"Oh yeah, Dad has been doing some of the cleaning," my brother said, scratching his head.

"Is he upset because I haven't done it?" I asked.

"No, I don't think so. I heard him say the other day that you've been working pretty hard at school and the hospital. He also said he suspected you had a lot on your mind, trying to get back into your ventriloquism and everything."

I bit my lip and stared out the window. *Maybe Dad does understand,* I mused. Maybe I haven't given him a fair shake after all. Red, blue, and gold neon lights from the highway flashed by.

Bryon reached over and patted my shoulder. "Well, anyway, I'm glad you found your dummy."

"Right. Ramblin' Rosie might be the only one who can pull Misty out of her weird mood." Yet an uncomfortable question haunted me—what if it doesn't work this time?

As the freeway stretched before us, darkness swallowed up each mile. At last we began twisting our way up the big hill that led to the hospital.

Leaving my brother in the visitor's lounge on the main floor, I caught the nearest elevator. As I approached the orthopedic ward, I heard a radio playing from the end of the hallway. Several interns were gathered near the nurses' station, talking in hushed tones.

Outside Misty's room, I recognized Mrs. Ebert lingering in the dimly lit hall. Her eyes were red and swollen, and she kept wiping them with a Kleenex.

"Oh, you must be Deanna," she said, looking up. "Mrs. Haddon told me you were coming. Shall I have her paged?"

"No. I'll go find her after I talk to Misty," I answered, trying to steady my voice.

"The operation's scheduled for Monday morning," Misty's mom explained haltingly. She sighed, glancing towards her daughter's room.

"Misty's probably scared," I said.

"Yes, but she never acted like this the last time."

"How long ago was that?" I asked.

"About a year and a half when they put the pin in her hip. I've tried hard to prepare her for the second surgery, but a lot has happened. The divorce . . . her favorite aunt dying . . . our move to Portland." Her words caught me by surprise. But on second thought, I had wondered why I'd never seen Misty's father.

Her lower lip quivered. "Oh Deanna, you've got to find out what's going on."

Instantly I felt as though someone had dumped the world's problems in my lap. With a nod, I squared my shoulders and slipped inside.

"Misty?" I said gently.

She looked at me with empty blue eyes, her lips pressed into a tight line.

"Misty, how are you?"

She turned her head away, and all I could see was the back of her tousled hair.

"I thought you might like some company tonight," I went on, sitting down on the edge of her bed. "If you don't feel like talking now, it's okay." I sucked in my breath, waiting for her to say or do something. When she didn't, I added, "I'd just like to be here with you for a while. Is that all right?"

"Uh-huh." She didn't turn around.

Looking for a way to fill the silence, I reached for Ramblin' Rosie. I straightened her dress. I smoothed her tousled hair. I placed her on my knee. But Misty still didn't look my way. What was I going to do now?

There was nothing left but to start wise-cracking with my dummy. If Misty didn't want to talk, well fine.

I knew it'd be wrong to try to force her. But maybe I could at least get her to smile.

Shyly she stole a glance in my direction. "Hi, Rambo Rosie," she murmured. My heart leaped.

"Hi, Misty Ebert." In my excitement, I forgot and moved my lips. Misty, eyes glued on Ramblin' Rosie, didn't seem to notice.

Then to my surprise, she pulled out from under the covers the paper bag clown puppet I'd made for her earlier. I never thought she'd keep it.

"My name's Smiley the Clown." She bounced the puppet in mid air.

"How nice to see you, Smiley." My dummy bowed. "Are you a circus clown?"

"I'm a sad clown. My friend Deanna said I love to laugh and tell silly stories, but she was wrong."

Eagerly I grabbed my cue. "Why was she wrong, Smiley the Clown?"

"Because she didn't know that sometimes clowns get sick and have operations and die . . . Sometimes they must go to a big hospital like Auntie Nan did. Sometimes they never come back."

I gasped. "Thinking about your Auntie Nan must make you feel bad," I made my dummy say.

Awkwardly she moved her puppet's mouth. "Uh-huh. It makes me feel really bad, but Auntie Nan wasn't my auntie. She belonged to Misty. Auntie Nan used to bring Misty red licorice to eat on Saturdays. And sometimes she took her to the movies or for an ice cream."

"Misty must miss her Auntie Nan," Ramblin' Rosie answered.

"She sure does! More than anything in the whole wide world."

A tear fell down Misty's face, spilling onto her covers. Still, she kept her puppet talking. "Rambo Rosie, I'm a sad clown because when I have my operation, I might never come back too. Then who would Misty play with?"

Chapter Nine

I couldn't take it any longer. I had to throw my arms around Misty and hold her. A minute later I handed her a Kleenex and struggled to keep my voice from shaking. "Misty, I want to tell you something. I heard the little talk our puppets just had."

"Me too."

I hesitated. "Will you do something for me?"

She eyed me skeptically. "Maybe. What?"

"Tell your clown that this hospital can be a wonderful place."

"My clown thinks it's a scary place."

I nodded. "Sometimes scary things happen in hospitals, things that make us hurt, things we don't understand." I hesitated again, searching for exactly the right words. This was even harder than trying to talk to Jason. "Nobody knew for sure Auntie Nan wouldn't come back," I went on. "But most of the time, people—er, puppets—get better in hospitals."

"Not all the time," she insisted.

I took her small hand in mine. "Misty, why do you suppose your clown never told her mommy the reason she feels so scared? She does have a mommy, doesn't she?"

"Yes, a very nice mommy. A nice clown mommy." She withdrew her hand from mine, then wrapped a corner of the blanket around her thumb. "That's the reason Smiley the Clown doesn't want her nice mommy to feel sad. She cries so much already. Ever since the clown's daddy went away and Auntie Nan died and all the other stuff."

I blinked back a tear. "Your puppet must talk to her mommy," I said simply. "She must tell her why she's scared. And I bet her mommy will tell her it's okay to be scared as long as she doesn't stop talking about it." I felt so phony. Though I was urging Misty to confide in her mother, I couldn't confide in mine. "That's what the doctors and nurses would tell her too," I added.

"Like Nurses Sarah and Melinda?"

I knew they were her favorites. "Yes, like Sarah and Melinda. And guess what?"

"What?"

"Sarah and Melinda and Doctor Morgan are going to take very good care of Smiley the Clown during her operation." I studied her solemn face. "Does this make any sense to you?"

"I think so."

"One more thing—something very important. Tell your puppet it's also all right to miss someone who's died or someone who's gone away. What's not all right is when we keep our loneliness locked up inside." I swallowed hard. "I know what that's like, Misty. I've done that too."

"And it gets more awful all the time?" she prompted.

"Yes, that's exactly what happens." Something inside of me seemed to melt. "Promise me you'll have a talk with Smiley the Clown?" I asked.

"I promise." She brightened. "Know something, Deanna? When I was four, I had an operation and it made me better. I'll tell my puppet that too."

"Terrific! Your puppet will be so glad." I hugged her again, feeling her wet cheek against mine. "I think there are some people who want to see you," I continued. "Like your mom and the nurses and Mrs. Haddon too. Shall I tell them it's okay now?"

"Uh-huh." She squirmed with anticipation, then smiled up at me. I felt as if someone had flooded the room with radiant sunshine.

The minute Bryon and I got home, I headed for the wastebasket and tore up my letter into little pieces.

If Misty could conquer her fears, then so could I. I'd go through with the show, no matter what. Then something hit me like a roaring avalanche: Misty and I weren't the only ones feeling scared. Without a doubt, every time my mother walked on stage, she was scared too.

I simply had to concentrate on my positive action even more. I sat down on my wicker chair and closed my eyes. It'd been so long since I'd last envisioned a positive me, I'd almost forgotten how.

Finally the picture came into focus. There I was, waiting behind the small stage in the hospital recreation room. My hair was dazzling, my smile captivating, and I was standing tall just like Mrs. Haddon had told me to.

Proudly I held Ramblin' Rosie at my side. A humongous crowd filled the room. Several reporters and photographers from the newspaper sat right in the front row. Even some anchormen from the biggest TV station in Portland were there!

The crowd murmured with anticipation. Then suddenly the lights went dim. Applause thundered as my dummy and I paraded onto the stage beneath a big floodlight. For the next few minutes, we took turns singing, tossed out jokes, and bombarded each other with wisecracks.

The people went wild! They clapped their hands, stomped their feet, cried out for more. It was wonderful, more wonderful than I'd ever dreamed possible. Then just after our third standing ovation, a Hollywood producer held out a contract and begged me to sign it on the spot. Gold pen in hand, I wrote my name on the dotted line. Again, the crowd roared with excitement!

Next my dad rushed up to me and smothered me in a hug. He told me how proud he was of me. He had tears of happiness in his eyes and . . . *Dad!* The thought of him snuffed out my daydream. Where was he anyway? I hadn't fixed him dinner, and now he was nowhere in sight. He'd probably retreated to the Elks Club to get something to eat.

I jumped up and rushed into the family room where my brother was working on his laptop. "Where's Dad?" I asked. I glanced at the clock above the fireplace mantel. It was nearly eleven.

"At the bowling alley. Why?"

"I've got to talk to him!"

"He'll probably be home in an hour."

"I can't wait that long. Will you take me there?" I pleaded.

My brother laughed. "Do I get chauffeur's pay? I swear, Deanna Lambert, all I've been doing tonight is running you around."

"Look, I'll pay for your gas with my baby-sitting money. I'll even make your favorite pumpkin pie. Anything you want. Just take me there!"

After Bryon had dropped me off inside the bowling alley, I spotted my father with a group of his friends. The rumble of balls striking down pins mingled with talking and laughter.

Quietly I slipped into a seat near the back. My dad had just scored a strike, and he appeared to be having a terrific time. I peered up at the scoreboard and discovered he'd made several strikes throughout the game. I couldn't remember seeing him this happy in a long time. Or had I been too wrapped up in my own problems to notice?

Unexpectedly I zeroed in on some people getting ready to leave. Sally and Kristy and three other kids were amongst them.

My heart started beating faster. I didn't want them to see me sitting there all by myself. Besides, I'd come to pay attention to Dad, and maybe when the game was over, pull him away from his friends for a long overdue talk. About Mom. About the three of us who were left—and all the things that really mattered. I couldn't afford to become sidetracked so soon.

To my relief, Sally and her friends disappeared out the front door.

Quickly I refocused my attention on the rest of Dad's game, then the one that followed. Each time, my dad bowled the highest score! I couldn't believe it. My father, the sour-faced old man, was vibrant and full of life.

When Dad finally discovered me sitting in the back row, his face lit up like a super charged light bulb.

"Deanna!" he exclaimed, clasping my shoulder. "How long have you been here?"

I smiled secretively. "Oh, at least an hour. You were terrific, Dad! I never realized . . ." I choked up and couldn't go on.

"You've been watching me for an hour? Just sitting here watching me?"

"Of course! Maybe next time I'll even join you."

I could see the happiness in his eyes, just like I'd seen it during my positive action session only minutes earlier. Suddenly it seemed as if I'd just pushed through a thick dark wall and discovered something wonderful on the other side.

"Dede, remember that banana split I tried to interest you in a while back? The kind I used to buy you when you were a little girl?" Dad stooped to untie his bowling shoes, then straightened, darting me a hopeful look.

"Sure," I answered.

"I still owe you one. Shall we make it a date? Maybe right now?"

I threw my arms around his broad neck. "You got it, Dad! Let's go."

Chapter Ten

"Oh no," I groaned. "Tammy, do you see what I see?"

I wanted to fold up into a little puff of vapor and disappear from the face of the earth. So what if the talent show was scheduled to begin in a mere twenty minutes? Now even my best friend's moral support wasn't good enough.

"What are you talking about?" She darted a look towards the large room behind the stage where the performers had congregated.

Two clowns dressed in rainbow-colored suits were standing by the door, practicing a juggling act. Another one was making funny faces into a mirror tacked on the wall.

"Got something against clowns?" she asked with an impish grin.

"Be serious!" I wailed. "You know what I'm talking about. How'd the drama club end up here?" I nodded towards the kids in costumes—a lion and several mice—who were filing through the door. Miss Beeson was bringing up the lead.

"Simple!" my friend exclaimed. "Mom needed more acts to round out the show so I suggested she call the drama club, and she did. Tonight they're performing *The Lion and the Mouse*. It's a take-off from *Androcles and the Lion*, the play they're putting on for the school next week."

"I know that," I answered. I'd already told myself I'd go to the play on opening night. "But why did the drama club have to end up here of all places?"

My insides were churning more than ever. How could I get up and perform in front of those kids after all the things that'd happened?

I watched the lion saunter about and practice a roar. The mice tittered and made dumb squeaking noises as they circled him.

"Some friend you are," I went on. "As if things aren't bad enough already. Now I'll really be the laugh of the century at school."

She waved her hands in exasperation and finally answered. "Deanna, calm down. You're making this sound like an all-time disaster."

"But it is! Don't forget, you promised to help me keep my ventriloquism quiet. It was your idea in the first place." I glanced again at the lion and the mice. "I suppose Sally and Jason and maybe even Kristy are in those costumes."

"Sure. Doesn't Kristy make a perfect lion?" Her pleased expression turned to a scowl. "Look, I know if you put your mind to it, you'll knock the socks off that audience—the drama kids included. You've got nothing to hide!"

I wasn't convinced, but I knew I had to give it my best shot. Chewing my fingernails, I peered down at my program. Mine was the first act. Maybe if I tried to ignore the kids from school, I thought desperately, they wouldn't realize it was me till I'd finished my act and made a quick get-away.

Seven fifty-five, the clock on the wall read. There was a big knot in my throat, and I clutched Ramblin' Rosie till my fingers turned white. I could almost hear the count-down. I wanted to turn and run. Yet the thought of Misty and Dad and Bryon sitting in the audience filled me with unexpected courage.

At last it was time to go on. I walked with Rosie onto the stage, my knees shaking.

"Thank you, thank you," I said haltingly into the microphone. I forced myself to smile as my gaze swept the audience. The many rows of folding chairs were filled. Kids too sick to sit on benches watched from wheelchairs and portable beds. And there was Misty, recovering from her operation, beaming at me from the front!

"Boys and girls, ladies and gentlemen." I swallowed hard. "My sidekick, Ramblin' Rosie and I are very pleased to be here with you tonight!"

"Sneezed, sneezed?" Ramblin' Rosie asked, blinking her round glassy eyes. "Who sneezed? I didn't hear anyone sneeze. Well, God bless you whoever you are!"

"No, no! Not sneezed. I said *pleased*!"

A chorus of giggles rose up from the kids in the audience.

Staring at my dummy, I forged ahead. "Ramblin' Rosie, I just told the audience that we're pleased to be here at Children's tonight. We're pleased to take part in this marvelous holiday talent show."

"You bet we are!" my dummy agreed. "Especially me!"

"Why especially you?"

"Because if I weren't here with all these nice boys and girls and moms and dads this evening, I'd probably be scrunched up in that ratty old carrying case you always keep me in."

"Why Ramblin' Rosie, I'm ashamed of you. That's not a ratty old carrying case. It's a super-duper deluxe piece of luggage! Genuine leather. The best in the West."

"Oh, yeah? Wanna bet? Is that why you told your Great Aunt Mildred you'd donate it to her once-a-year garage sale? The one where nothing ever sells!"

She doubled-over with mock laughter.

I heaved a sigh. "Ramblin' Rosie, you're impossible. I never said that to Great Aunt Mildred. Now settle down and lend me your ear. I've got a joke for you and all the boys and girls in the audience."

She moaned. "Oh no, not another one of your dumb jokes!"

"Sure! This one's terrific. Are you ready? Now listen carefully."

She turned his back in a gesture of defiance.

My voice grew louder. "I said, Ramblin' Rosie, are you ready to hear my terrific joke?"

Still no answer.

I looked out at the audience and spotted Dad and Bryon grinning at me from near the back. "Boys and girls, ladies and gentlemen, apparently Ramblin' Rosie has some difficulty hearing me tonight. I need your help. Now at the count of three, we'll all say together: *Are you ready, Ramblin' Rosie?*"

The children in the front row eagerly nodded their heads. Some of the others called out in excited exclamations.

"Altogether now. One. Two. Three. Are you ready, Ramblin' Rosie?" A chorus of eager high-pitched voices joined mine.

My dummy continued to look away.

"Okay, everyone, we'll have to try it again! Don't forget to sing it out loud and clear." I lead them in another hearty chorus.

Children giggled, some clapped their hands with delight, and others cheered. All eyes were fixed on my dummy's face, not mine.

"Come on, Ramblin' Rosie!" a small voice sang out.

A victorious feeling bubbled up inside of me. At that very moment, I knew the magic was beginning. The kids believed Ramblin' Rosie lived and breathed just like them.

Finally my dummy faced the audience and said, "I hear you! I hear you!" Then turning to me, she continued, "Okay, Miss Deanna. Lay it on me."

I cleared my throat. "Well, it's about time. Here goes. Are you ready?"

"Ready!"

"What did the 500-pound mouse say to the cat?"

"Find me some cheese."

"Wrong. Guess again."

"Don't step on my tail."

"Still wrong."

Ramblin' Rosie dipped her head. "All right, Miss Deanna. I give up. What did the 500-pound mouse say to the cat?"

"Here kitty, kitty, kitty."

As the audience roared with laughter, my spirits soared. The dream was working! I wanted to laugh and cry and dance all at the same time. With a start, I thought about my mother. Maybe her dream was working too.

For the next several minutes, Ramblin' Rosie and I carried on with more jokes and insults. I even pulled off my final trunk act without one mistake! Everyone loved it.

After I was done, I decided to stick around for the entire program—the clown juggling act, a youth choir singing Christmas carols, a five-member rock band, and finally *The Lion and the Mouse*. It didn't matter anymore if the kids from school teased me. I was simply feeling too good about what I'd accomplished.

Back stage, Mrs. Haddon swept me up in a hug. "You were fabulous! I knew you could do it! Oh, Deanna, I'm so proud."

"Thanks," I answered, too moved to say more. Soon we were joined by Dad and Bryon. Then came Miss Beeson and Sally and Jason and all the rest.

"Hey," Sally said, smiling widely. "Way to go! Why didn't you let us know you were into ventriloquism?"

I shrugged, embarrassed and happy all at the same time.

"You should join the drama club," Jason said, nudging my side. He winked. "Of course, the competition might be a little tough, but after seeing your performance tonight, I think you could crack through it."

Everyone laughed good-naturedly. This time I was laughing with them.

"I might just do that," I answered. A new thrill washed over me. I was accepted. Part of the crowd. The author of my positive action book really knew what she was talking about.

"The activities bus is stopping for pizza on the way home," Sally continued. "We'd love to have you and Tammy come along. Besides, it'll give you a chance to get to know us better. I, for one, really hope you decide to join our club."

I looked hesitantly over at Dad.

"Go with them, Dede," he gently urged. "You've more than earned it. And besides, it's about time you had some fun. "

"But what about Rosie?" I didn't want to drag her with me onto a crowded school bus that was headed to the pizza place.

"I'll be glad to take her home." Dad winked at me. "After a night like tonight, I think she's more than ready to hit the hay."

Breaking into a smile, I nodded in agreement. I was thrilled that Dad was taking such a personal interest in my dummy.

I inhaled deeply and finally said to Sally. "Thanks! I'd love to go with all of you for pizza. I think Tammy will too." Even the thought of struggling with stringy mozzarella cheese couldn't change my mind. I knew now I was among friends.

A flash of chrome caught my attention, and I spotted Misty's mother pushing her up to me in a small-sized wheelchair. I reached down to kiss the little girl's flushed forehead.

Misty burst into a big smile as she held out her clown puppet up for me to see. "Happy the Clown is going to get well, Deanna!" she cried. "Her operation's all over!"

"Oh, yes, I know that!" I answered, squeezing her shoulder. "And I'm so happy, Misty. This is a great night all of us!"

"Deanna . . ."

"Yes, Misty?"

"Are you coming to see me Saturday?"

"You bet I am. Why?"

"I've got something to show you!" she proclaimed. "A brand-new doll. Almost like Ramblin' Rosie! She's so special."

I looked at her mother questioningly. "A real dummy," she supplied with an even smile. "I found it at a toy store in Portland. Of course, Smiley the Clown will always be number one, but we decided the puppet needed another friend." Her eyes gleamed. "And who knows, this new friend might become a star someday. Just like Ramblin' Rosie!"

I was still smiling as I watched Misty's mother wheel her out of the room. Dad and Bryon walked alongside them, telling the little girl about my famous great-grandfather ventriloquist. The next time I visited her, Misty would be brimming with new questions.

Yes, what a night, I thought with a sigh. I wanted to pinch myself to make sure it wasn't another dream.

"Jason, don't forget to pass out our publicity signs before everyone leaves." The sound of Miss Beeson's voice jolted me out of my thoughts. She waved an oversized manila envelope before his face as she shrugged into her green wool coat.

"Oh, that's right, Miss Beeson," Jason answered. "Thanks for reminding me." He looked over at me. "Hey, Deanna. Don't run away. This will only take a minute." He tucked the envelope under his arm. "On second thought, come with me."

Hesitantly, I tagged alongside of him. I couldn't believe he really wanted me hanging around.

"Miss Beeson put me in charge of this fund raiser weeks ago," he explained. "The official starting date is tomorrow morning."

I stared down at one of the signs and caught my breath. Boldly printed words seemed to jump out at me: *Guess What I'm Doing After School Today?* It was exactly like the sign Jason has slapped on my back that humiliating day by my locker!

"Fund raiser!" I exclaimed as he handed a sign to Jodie Gomez, one of the mice in the skit. "What fund raiser?"

"The one the drama club is sponsoring to raise extra money for field trips. Each of us will wear a sign on our back all day at school to let everyone know we're drumming up business. We're hoping to run errands, baby-sit, collect newspapers for recycling—any way we can raise the money."

My jaw dropped. I looked at Jason and said, "But I thought when you pinned that sign on my back, you were making fun of me!"

"Making fun of you? What for?"

"Because I was spending my time after school practicing with my dummy." My face grew hot. "I made Tammy—and my brother Bryon—swear they wouldn't let anyone at school know I was into ventriloquism. But after I saw your sign, I was positive that's what it was all about. I just knew everyone at school was laughing behind my back."

He grinned sheepishly. "I can tell we need to talk. Hold on. This will only take a minute more." One by one he handed out the rest of the posters while I waited close by, feeling like a fool.

Now I've really blown it, I thought. I hadn't meant to get so carried away with my explanation. Who would've ever believed I'd once been tongue-tied around Jason?

"Let's go outside," he suggested when he'd finally finished. "The bus won't leave for a while yet."

We hurried though the door marked exit onto a graveled walkway. As my eyes adjusted to the darkness, I noticed a scattering of stars winking from an inky blue sky.

Jason spoke guardedly. "Deanna, about that sign. I guess I was sort of teasing you. But it's not like you think. I wanted to get your attention, and I wasn't sure how to do it. Anyway, I'd been working on these signs for the fund raiser, and I figured if I put one on your back, it'd be sort of like an ice-breaker. Most of all, I wanted to get to know you better. I guess now it was kind of dumb, but I didn't know how else to do it." He shrugged his shoulders and added, "I never dreamed you were so talented. You and Ramblin' Rosie gave the coolest performance in this entire talent show tonight. You two are a team! You're gonna be super stars!"

"Thanks," I said simply. His praise made my heart soar as I thought back to his confession about being afraid to talk to me. Were my ears playing tricks on me? Still, I could see now I'd been so busy trying to hide my secret, I'd jumped to conclusions. Tammy had told me I was getting carried away, and I guess she was right.

The sounds of shrieks and laughter filled the parking lot. A full moon cast gauzy ribbons of white light across our pathway, and the crisp night air stung my cheeks. Not far away, the school bus stood waiting while the kids started to climb on.

As I walked with Jason towards the bus, I made a silent promise. Tomorrow, first thing before I started my chores, I'd write a long e-mail to Mom. I'd write about finding something special . . . about feeling scared . . . about plunging ahead anyhow.

Maybe she'd understand. Just like—maybe someday—I'd better understand her reason for leaving. It might take a long, long time. Years, perhaps. But somehow I could tell that first shred of light was beginning to poke through.

The End

Don't miss out!

Visit the website below and you can sign up to receive emails whenever Sydell Lowell Voeller publishes a new book. There's no charge and no obligation.

https://books2read.com/r/B-A-KKZY-ENWYC

BOOKS 2 READ

Connecting independent readers to independent writers.

About the Author

Sydell Lowell Voeller grew up in Edmonds, Washington, and has lived in Forest Grove, Oregon for many years. Her family consists of a husband, two grown sons and their wives, and four grandchildren.

Sydell has been a violinist in semiprofessional orchestras, a registered nurse, and a writing instructor for the LongRidge Writer's Institute. Her interests include reading, camping, astronony, crafting, astronomy, and playing with her two cats.